Sherlock Holmes and the
Mystery of the Forgotten Password

Bruno Vincent is the author of more than thirty books, which have been translated into fifteen languages. He is best known for the Enid Blyton for Grown Ups series (in which he introduced the Famous Five to the perils of modern life), ten of which were *Sunday Times* bestsellers. He has contributed to serious works about the history of poetry and literature, but has also written humorous books in the voices of Charles Dickens, Prince Harry and Danger Mouse, as well as his own collections of horror stories for children, *Grisly Tales from Tumblewater* and *School for Villains.*

Sherlock Holmes and the Mystery of the Forgotten Password

BRUNO VINCENT

**PENGUIN
VIKING**

VIKING

UK | USA | Canada | Ireland | Australia
India | New Zealand | South Africa

Viking is part of the Penguin Random House group of companies
whose addresses can be found at global.penguinrandomhouse.com.

Penguin Random House UK,
One Embassy Gardens, 8 Viaduct Gardens, London sw11 7bw

penguin.co.uk
global.penguinrandomhouse.com

First published 2024

001

Copyright © Bruno Vincent, 2024

Set in 12.5/14.75pt Garamond MT Std
Typeset by Jouve (UK), Milton Keynes
Printed and bound in Great Britain by Clays Ltd, Elcograf S.p.A.

The authorized representative in the EEA is Penguin Random House Ireland,
Morrison Chambers, 32 Nassau Street, Dublin D02 YH68

A CIP catalogue record for this book is available from the British Library

ISBN: 978-0-241-72148-3

I

It was a fine day in August, the sky over London bright blue after a night of storms. At Baker Street I had the pleasure of receiving an honoured and respected guest.

'You always did make a good cup of tea, Dr Watson,' said Inspector Lestrade. Which is to say, Vicky Lestrade, daughter of our old Scotland Yard associate.

'How is your dear father?' I asked. 'Retirement treats him well, I trust?'

'He's on great form,' said Vicky. 'Golf, birdwatching – and he's forever going on holiday, visiting ancient ruins. Speaking of which, Dr Watson . . . how is our friend the consulting detective?'

'Ah,' I said, cradling my cup in my hands. 'Difficult to answer – Holmes is such an unpredictable fellow. Recently, you see, it's become impossible to deny that he's . . .' I lowered my voice. '. . . *on the spectrum*.'

Vicky nodded sagely, and at that same moment the living-room door crashed open. In strode Holmes in a state of wild excitement. In his hand was a piece of electronic equipment which I believe is termed a 'joystick'.

'Watson!' he cried. 'This Sinclair ZX Spectrum is a marvellous piece of equipment! What will those clever fellows at Silicon Valley think of next? I've been hard at work all morning and I've not allowed a single space invader to reach the surface of the earth!'

'I know that Mrs Hudson uses something called "detergent"
and another thing called "conditioner". Beyond that, it is as
baffling a mystery to me as any I've encountered.'

2

'Oh, hello Victoria,' said Holmes, seeing we had company. He stood up straight and put his hands behind his back – hiding the joystick. 'What brings you to these parts?'

'Sherlock,' said Inspector Lestrade, with a cautious smile. Like many of the younger generation, she frequently found Holmes superior and patronizing, and more than a little out of touch – but could not help being fond of him, like a troublesome uncle.

'I thought I'd pop in because I was in the neighbourhood,' she said. 'Another one of those anonymous pieces of street art appeared overnight – right here on Baker Street! They're a nightmare for us: roads blocked while people take pictures, and others try to deface them, and so forth.'

'Really,' said Holmes. 'Doesn't this Banksy fellow get bored of doing the same thing over and over? All this skulking around under the cover of darkness – you'd think by his age he'd want to stay at home and take up an easel?'

'Actually, it's not him,' said Lestrade, getting up. 'In fact you can just see the artwork from here, if you look carefully.'

'Ah yes,' I said, following her pointing finger. 'I did wonder what the commotion was about. This person only leaves mysterious blocky stencils, I understand. Rather like a computer image. Not a million miles away from one of the games on your beloved Spectrum, Holmes . . .'

'Never mind that, Watson,' Holmes muttered. 'Now, this pattern – I see it everywhere. What is it?'

'It's called a QR code,' said Vicky Lestrade. 'When you hold your phone's camera in front of it, you are automatically taken to a web address. At first people thought these were just graffiti. But word has been spreading that for the *first* person to scan them, it's a very different story indeed – they unlock a huge sum of money, in the hundreds of thousands of pounds!'

'What!' said Holmes. 'You mean we had a fortune going begging under our noses, if only we'd realized? What are you playing at, Watson, missing such an opportunity?'

'Certainly not the Sinclair Spectrum, Holmes,' I said.

'Well, quite!' said Holmes. 'With that money I could upgrade to an Amstrad. Or a Commodore 64!'

3

'Before you get too excited, these moneys – if the story is true – are only payable in cryptocurrency,' said Lestrade. 'So you'd have to get your heads round that first.'

'Then I've no interest,' said Holmes, turning away. He hefted the teapot to see how full it was, and hunted for a cup. 'I'll be long in my grave before anyone manages to explain all that twaddle to me.'

'Sounds to me like a financial matter, Inspector,' I said. 'Should you not get the Financial Crimes Division to look into it?'

'A very good idea,' said Vicky Lestrade. 'In fact – you know there's an epidemic of ransomware attacks in the country right now?'

I expected another baffled expostulation from Holmes, but to my surprise he responded eagerly: 'Yes, I've heard of those. Someone breaks into a company and steals all their internal information, holding it to ransom for exorbitant sums of money?'

'That's right,' said Vicky. 'It's happening so often, the Met set up a brand-new Ransomware Response Unit to deal with them.'

'Good idea!' I said. 'The Metropolitan Police getting ahead of the game for once.'

'Unfortunately, on the first day of operations, they were hit with a massive ransomware attack. And had to shut down.'

4

'Ah,' said Holmes. 'Most unfortunate.'

'Yeah, so all the money's gone and it's all hands to the pump again.'

'Well,' said Holmes. 'Keep your eyes peeled for these artworks, and perhaps you can get some of the money back.'

'Where have these – what do you call them? Graffiti? – appeared?' I asked.

'All over the world,' said Lestrade. 'Bangladesh, Washington DC, Jakarta . . . People are trying to work out if there's a pattern to the locations, and also wondering about the motive of whoever it is who's doing it.'

'Sounds like a modern Robin Hood at work,' said Holmes.

'Hmmph,' said Lestrade, unimpressed. 'More likely to be a guerrilla marketing campaign for Richstream.'

'Richstream?' asked Holmes and myself in one voice.

'Oh, really, you two might as well be living under a rock! Richstream – the cryptocurrency that's quickly replacing Bitcoin. It's promoted by that billionaire creep who's everywhere these days – Igor Glebe. The berk who wants to put a computer chip in everyone's brains, god help us. Anyway, that's the currency being given away by our mysterious artist. Possibly they – like everyone else who invested in Richstream – have made a mint and want to give something back . . .'

'Has any actual crime been committed, though?' I asked. 'Besides defacement of private property, which is easy enough to put right?'

'It's disruptive to public order, and a headache for me personally,' said Vicky. 'But more than that – giving away millions of quid. I mean, it's just damn *suspicious*, don't you think?'

Sherlock Holmes did not respond. He had taken a handwritten letter from the mantelpiece and was staring fixedly at it.

'Is it Wednesday today?' he asked, spinning round. We told him it was.

'I *am* getting scatterbrained these days,' he said quietly. 'Thank goodness you mentioned this Igor Glebe fellow – for Watson and I are due to meet him this very lunchtime! Did I neglect to tell you, Watson? Well, well, you have my apologies – but we must make haste to Waterloo station. Forgive us, Inspector, but now I must change!'

He zoomed out of the room precipitately, tossing his joystick onto the divan. Lestrade and I exchanged a look.

'I don't think he'll ever change,' she said.

A brisk walk to Baker Street Underground station, and one clattering tube journey later, Holmes and I were on a train as it glided through the English shires.

'And what happens if you lose that precious device of

'But surely you understand: just because we are in a smoking carriage, that doesn't mean you *have* to smoke!'

yours?' Holmes asked, tucking his paper ticket into his top pocket as we took our seats. My ticket was electronic and saved to my phone – in the form of what I now knew was called a QR code.

'I would replace it, Holmes. All these things are backed up, you know. On the . . . the Cloud, and suchlike,' I said vaguely.

But discussion of technology caused Holmes's eyes to glaze over. He settled into his seat, steepled his fingers over his long aquiline nose and appeared to go into a doze. Then he said quietly: 'Tell me what you know about our host this afternoon. The world-famous Mr Glebe.'

'Ah yes,' I said. 'I've been looking into him. Igor Glebe – a most extraordinary fellow. Richest person in England by a country mile.'

'A couple of billion country miles, I should say,' said Holmes.

'Perhaps the richest person in the world. He is the CEO of a very large medical technology company, called EGO. Their famous motto – which one sees in advertising everywhere – is "Be Better". They make the GEN: a patch which monitors people's health and dietary requirements, warns of disease symptoms, and releases doses of drugs, supplements and minerals into the bloodstream. His company doubled in value last week when he teased that the latest of his life-saving devices is nearly ready.'

'This new product of theirs is known as the "NEXT-GEN" device, I believe?' Holmes murmured without opening his eyes.

'Indeed – it is apparently a brain implant, as Vicky mentioned this morning. The public are naturally suspicious of such a thing. But it's the *possibilities* that make people so passionate, you see, Holmes,' I said. 'It may prevent or even reverse dementia, detect intolerances, control seizures – and those are just the medical aspects. Imagine buying things or writing emails just by thinking about them. All via the careful electronic stimulation of parts of the brain. Think of it, Holmes – you'd never forget another password!'

'I don't forget passwords now,' said Holmes loftily, 'because I refuse to have them in the first place. Dashed impudent, demanding we keep passwords for every last thing!'

I glanced doubtfully at him. I wondered if he was telling an outright fib – or whether he had somehow forgotten the amazing frequency with which he failed to remember passwords. I decided to gloss over it.

'You don't forget passwords, Holmes, because you have a Watson who keeps track of them for you,' I said quietly, patting my notebook and recalling that, a few hours earlier, he'd seemed unsure which day it was.

Holmes made no sign of hearing me. 'But, *brain implants* – it ought to have taken decades of research to get to such a point,' he said. 'The company's not been going for a handful of years. I mean, experimenting by cutting into human brains, for goodness' sake . . .'

'I tell you, Holmes, if a quarter of what people are speculating about regarding the device's capabilities turns out to be right, it could indeed be a real turning point in human history.'

'Big talk, Watson,' Holmes scoffed. '*Enormous* talk! Time will tell.'

6

'I wonder what this Glebe fellow wants to talk to *us* about, though, Watson,' Holmes said as the train rocketed happily past Basingstoke. 'Tell me what you know of the man himself.'

'Indeed,' I said. 'Igor Glebe. Forty-one years of age. Blond, handsome, athletic. Little is known of his personal history – he arrived on the world stage seemingly from nowhere. Made his money building up a cryptocurrency exchange. Which I confess I do not understand . . .'

'Richstream again?' said Holmes. I nodded. 'There's something about that name which irks me . . .'

'Then, four years ago, he purchased the company which makes the GEN personal health device, and changed the company name to EGO. That was when he appeared in public for the first time.'

'No one had heard of him until then?' asked Holmes.

'Not other than as a name on a screen, I believe. He was homeschooled on a farm in the Australian Outback by religious parents – both of whom have passed away,' I said. 'But although he came from obscurity, he quickly made a name for himself. He's irascible and rude with journalists, and makes wild, outlandish and aggressive statements on social media, apparently just for the amusement of it.'

'Sounds unstable,' said Holmes.

'There is a cult of personality around the man,' I said. 'The more unstable he appears, the more his fans cheer and say it is all a game he is playing. Whether he's mocking someone with a disability, or challenging a prime minister to a boxing match.'

'The afternoon is looking up, then!' said Holmes. 'Perhaps he wants to see if he can last a few rounds in the ring with Sherlock Holmes!'

'Holmes, I wish you would be serious.'

'I'm a tad rusty, I confess,' Holmes grumbled. 'But there's still plenty of force in my famous left jab, I assure you!'

He was still practising this supposedly celebrated manoeuvre as the train eased into the tiny station of Tubmouth. A slim young woman waited on the platform, seeming anxious and distracted.

'Mr Holmes!' she said, as we disembarked. 'I'm Jenny Yuen, Mr Glebe's assistant. I'm so glad you're here. You see, Igor Glebe has disappeared!'

7

Within moments we were in a car and speeding towards the EGO estate.

Jenny Yuen had an open, appealing manner, but was highly distracted under the stress of the current circumstances.

'Tell us all,' said Holmes, soothingly. 'No – wait. First tell me this. It was Mr Glebe's personal idea to invite me here? And he chose the day?'

'Yes – yes he did,' she said.

'That is well. Please proceed.'

'When I went to his apartment this morning, he wasn't there,' she said. I noticed that she was not in the slightest flustered at being spoken to commandingly (and perhaps imperiously) by an older male. I wondered if this shed some light on her relationship with her employer.

'There was a storm last night,' she said. 'Some cables came down over the property, and there was other damage. Part of the outer wall was crushed by a falling tree. But when I came to collect him for the morning meetings, his bed had not been slept in.'

'Has he absconded before?' asked Holmes.

'Of course not!' Ms Yuen seemed offended by this question, which sounded to me like a reasonable one. Holmes's eyes and my own met for a moment.

'So you are afraid for his safety, then,' Holmes said.

'I honestly don't know what to think,' she replied. 'He's a *very* important person. He's in charge of one of the biggest companies on earth, when it's about to really change the world to *be better*. Everything we've done before this was just preamble. The whole mission, to improve life on earth, is within our reach . . .'

'Might he have been kidnapped?' I asked. 'You have received no ransom demands?'

She shook her head. 'Not yet. And I mean . . . *how*? Our compound is utterly protected and surveilled. More efficiently than most prisons, in fact – our technology is worth billions. No one saw him leave. No one saw anything.'

'Then both the method and the motive of his disappearance are equally mysterious,' said Sherlock Holmes.

8

The car swung in through arched security gates and up a ribbon of asphalt through manicured green pastures. We were driven through a widely spaced complex of precisely geometrical buildings in bright colours.

Here was an orange box, there a yellow pyramid. Further on were a baby-pink sphere and a red cylinder. They were as architecturally alien to the English landscape as a fridge-freezer in the centre of a Rembrandt.

As we climbed from the car we saw how vast the brightly coloured hulks were. Each was perhaps three hundred feet high, and we were informed that the campus as a whole was home to thousands of employees.

'One feels ant-like, standing in this technological Valley of the Kings,' said Holmes.

We were taken directly to Igor Glebe's living quarters, a rhubarb-coloured rhombus on a rise of land with a commanding view towards the distant English Channel, abutted by an octagonal swimming pool.

At the front door we were confronted by a colossal security official, his muscular form further swollen by clusters of snap-lock pockets containing vaguely threatening machinery.

'Eugene Kostak,' he said with a curt nod in our general direction. 'Unfortunate you have been inconvenienced like this. We will put you on the next train to London.'

They were horrified to see how built up Clapham
was getting these days.

Jenny Yuen opened her mouth to protest, but Sherlock Holmes beat her to it.

'You will do no such thing,' said Holmes gaily. 'Send away the world's finest detective, *because* you have an unsolved mystery? I've never heard of anything so absurd.'

'This is an internal security matter . . .' Kostak said darkly. 'It's not appropriate—'

'No,' said Jenny Yuen. 'Eugene! I think you are overlooking one – at least one – very important factor.'

I noticed with approval that the diminutive Ms Yuen was as comfortable giving orders to powerful men as she was receiving them. Kostak was not someone I would cheerfully gainsay under the best of circumstances. He turned his bulk in her direction with heavy reluctance.

'And what is that?' he asked.

'Mr Glebe deliberately invited Mr Holmes to come here *today*. The same day he's gone missing. It seems obvious he knew something was going to happen – and that he intended Mr Holmes to investigate!'

9

'Atta girl!' said Holmes. 'You took the words right out of my mouth!'

Holmes looked so pleased with himself I worried he might add 'so put that in your pipe' or offer the security guard a playful exemplar of the famous left jab. Kostak regarded us all with misgiving, but decided that for the moment he was not in a position to argue. He moved inside and showed us Glebe's apartment.

The rooms were spacious and grand, without (to my eye) being either appealing or characterful. There were works of art on the walls (Ms Yuen explained to us) which were of a value that was astonishing – not to say actually unbelievable, as the artworks were largely indistinguishable from the surrounding furnishings.

Holmes made a minute inspection of the entire apartment, but I could see frustration in his every movement.

'This place is absolutely and utterly clean, and absent of any physical evidence that I can see,' he said, a short while into his inspection. 'I feel as though it might have been newly constructed this morning.'

'It is cleaned six times a day,' said Ms Yuen.

'Six!' I ejaculated. 'Is that not a little overzealous?'

'I never thought about it before,' she confessed. 'You get used to some strange things, when you live with the ultra-rich.'

'There are cameras everywhere,' Holmes observed. 'May we see the footage?'

Kostak did not like this, but he led us out along a path, and then into a nearby construction (a magenta trapezium) where screens completely blanketed the walls. Smartly dressed minions by the score busied themselves at workstations in every corner of available space. They appeared to me to be in a frenzy of activity, casting hardly a glance in our direction.

'I'm interested in the hours before he left, of course,' said Holmes.

'His personal rooms are monitored at all times?' I asked wonderingly.

'Of course,' said Kostak. 'By Glebe's own orders,' he added.

Kostak turned to talk quietly to one of his buzzing factotums, who pressed a series of buttons, and the screen in front of us turned blank. 'Be Better', the company's tagline, glowed in the corner.

'There's nothing,' said the employee, perplexed.

'That's not right,' Kostak said, looking more intense and grave by the second. 'There must be a back-up . . .'

'It was disabled . . .' said the technician.

'When is the last footage of Mr Glebe that we *do* have?' asked Holmes.

There was some muttering, and manipulation of software. At last an image came up. In it, a tall athletic man was sitting at a computer terminal in his private rooms.

'This is the last thing before the blackout,' said the employee. 'It's from last night at 22.17.'

'Winds were blowing about eighty miles an hour at this

point,' said Kostak. 'We already had some flooding in the staff facilities.'

'What's he doing?' asked Holmes.

'Holmes, he's accessing his computer – surely you can see that?' I said.

'No he isn't, Watson,' said Holmes. 'Quite the reverse. Why, it's as clear as day the man has forgotten his password!'

There was a momentary pause. Then everyone looked at the screen again, as the footage replayed.

Before anyone could stop him, Holmes leant forward and unpinched the screen, zooming right in on the keyboard as Glebe typed.

'Hey!' barked Kostak. 'That's not—'

'Mr Kostak,' said Holmes steadily. 'No one poses less of a threat to the security of your little empire than I do . . . Unless your systems are vulnerable to attack from a ZX Spectrum . . .'

No one was listening. They all watched the screen as Glebe typed a third time, and then hammered on the counter beside the keyboard with his fist.

Everyone in the room could see that Sherlock Holmes was right.

This was too much of a strain upon the authority of the mighty Kostak. Making excuses that information had to be carefully analysed, and saying something about security clearances, he ushered us out and closed the door.

'No doubt to continue observing us from within, Watson,' said Holmes quietly into my ear. 'Now, my dear helpful Ms Yuen,' he said more loudly. 'Let us look at the damage from the storm last night. You said the perimeter walls were breached?'

We quickly reached the spot where a tree had fallen and crushed the outer wall. Impressively, tree surgeons had already dismembered it, and piled the logs in the back of a flatbed truck, while a foreman was directing half a dozen construction workers in mending the fabric of the wall.

'Mightily efficient,' said Holmes. 'I say, why not taste the fresh air *outside* the EGO premises. I don't like being fenced in – do you, Ms Yuen? Care for a walk?'

She acquiesced, and together we made a circuit around the entire grounds, getting our shoes thoroughly muddy in the process, but learning a great deal from the enthusiastic assistant to the Great Man, Igor Glebe.

To say that Jenny Yuen admired her employer was an understatement. She found him as magnificent as she did impossible. She gave me the impression of not quite understanding him – but feeling compelled to try, and fulfilled by the effort.

She told us how he had set up offices all over the world – Hong Kong, Dubai, the Pacific republic of San Colombo – but had a reputation for hundred-hour work weeks and never leaving the office. That was all until the company's relocation to England, however.

'He suddenly changed,' she said. 'He seemed happier but unhappier at the same time. He went to a traditional English pub and paid for everyone's drinks for the whole month! He paid for the repairs to a medieval church roof, out of his own pocket. A hundred thousand pounds – without batting an eyelid!'

'It seems peaceful on campus,' said Holmes. 'The

large majority of employees do not know of his disappearance yet?'

We had reached the stump of the tree which had fallen and crushed the EGO outer wall. It had been an energetic tramp, up- and downhill, over several miles of muddy countryside.

Holmes sat on the stump, and scraped mud from his shoes against the roots while I gratefully leant against the wall for a moment to catch my breath.

'No!' she said. 'And they mustn't. Please respect that. It's still so early – we have no idea what's happening. News getting out could destroy the company, and may risk thousands of jobs needlessly . . .'

'You trust this man,' observed Holmes, looking out across the English countryside. 'Despite his wild political opinions, his erratic behaviour . . .'

'That's not what he's truly like,' she said. 'I know him in person and he's kind and thoughtful. Funny and sincere. That's his online personality, not the *real him*. Not the boss I know . . .' She hesitated, and seemed to suffer some inward conflict. Looking at her out of the corner of my eye I thought I saw Jenny Yuen nerve herself for some kind of admission, but then her courage seemed to fail her. I saw Holmes, too, regarding her slyly.

'Oh, ignore me, I've said too much . . .'

'Not a bit,' said Holmes. 'Everything you just said is of crucial importance. Now, young Jenny – is that a fresh storm brewing, or is it my rumbling stomach? I was rather hoping to find out that real-life billionaires genuinely eat "billionaire's shortbread". But the EGO refectory seems only to serve rustic peasant food, all leaves and lentils. What say you we journey to this local pub you spoke of, and have ourselves a good old-fashioned spot of lunch?'

'Yes, that was amazing,' said the barmaid at the Dog and Star pub. 'Just imagine, buying drinks for everyone, for a whole month! I mean – it's been a nightmare, of course! But it made us kind of famous. Exciting to have someone so well known in our quiet little pub. He's taller than you think. And more handsome . . .'

The barmaid in question was a sharp-nosed blonde woman in her mid-twenties, with the swift and brisk manner of the hyper-competent. Except, that is, when dreamily reminiscing about Igor Glebe. Jenny Yuen eyed her with hostility, as Holmes carried our drinks to a table in the corner.

'When was this pub visit?' Holmes asked.

'Two Tuesdays ago,' said Jenny. 'Twelve forty-five p.m. Although we arrived two minutes late.'

'There you are, Watson,' he said. 'We like witnesses to be accurate, and you can't ask for more than that! Now, watch out – there's paint on your coat from when you brushed against the outer wall of the EGO compound earlier . . .'

I examined my coat in horror to find this was indeed the case. In embarrassment, I ineffectually dabbed the sleeve with napkins before folding the coat up, marvelling – here was efficiency, indeed! The wall had been damaged not so many hours ago, and here it was already repainted! I cursed my ill chance while Holmes's questioning went on.

'Ms Yuen, you are admirably precise and accurate – and, I have no doubt, an assistant nonpareil. It is your job to notice things others miss, and to anticipate. So,' Holmes said, 'what do you think has happened here?'

Her face went blank. She took a sip of ginger ale. And, uncomfortable under our joint gazes, looked out of the window. Traffic swished past on the country road. The sky was blue and distant, as though the whole world was taking a peaceful breath after the exhaustion of the storm.

We were all distracted by a loud mention of the missing man's name at the next table. Holmes and I turned to listen while some delighted locals toasted Glebe's taste in football teams.

'Pardon me butting in,' said Holmes, 'but am I to understand Mr Glebe made a local sporting investment?'

Two middle-aged men assented over their pints of lager and plates of scampi and chips.

'I've never laughed so hard in my life,' said one. 'Tubmouth & Crettingdean – the crappest football team imaginable. Round here we call them the Tubby Cretins. And this billionaire prat says he's going to take them to the top of the Premier League!'

'Indeed!' said Holmes, turning back to Jenny. 'So he is a sports enthusiast. Was this another whim? A practical joke?' he asked.

She shook her head. 'No – it's not like his other pranks . . .'

'You mean like when he said he'd buy the moon and sell advertising space on it? Or offered to play Vladimir Putin at Twister? Might one of these pranks,' Holmes suggested, holding up his glass of claret and squinting analytically into it, 'involve disappearing for a few days, and getting the "great Sherlock Holmes" to investigate? For his own amusement?'

'I can see why you might think that,' said Ms Yuen. 'But this . . .' She met Holmes's eye. 'It's different. I can feel it. I don't know how I know. But he's gone.' Suddenly she seemed close to tears. 'And I'm afraid he's not coming back!'

Holmes had a decidedly relaxed attitude to anyone
requesting to borrow one of his books.

Holmes examined the enthusiastic (and, it seemed clear to me, besotted) assistant over a sombre and thoughtful ploughman's lunch. When she had excused herself to the bathroom, the barmaid came to collect the empties.

'When Glebe was here that day,' Holmes said as she picked up the glasses, 'there was a slight awkwardness, was there not? Someone had a few too many drinks, I seem to recall . . .'

She frowned for a second, then remembered something.

'That drunk girl!' she said. 'I'd forgotten. The EGO people obviously wanted to turn the visit into a photo opportunity, and she kind of blundered in and spoilt it. He was super-gracious about it. But yeah – god. Fancy being that drunk at *lunchtime*.'

'Do you remember what she looked like, this drunk person? Did you have to escort her out?'

'Not really,' she said. 'It's funny, I didn't see her face, that I remember. Just some middle-aged office worker, I guess. After she bumped into him she must have left of her own accord . . .'

'Thank you,' said Sherlock Holmes. 'You have been most helpful. Now, young Jenny,' he said to the returning assistant. 'Watson has shown me on his map telephone thingy that this church roof Mr Glebe paid for is nearby. May we perhaps visit it?'

By now it was clear that there must be very important matters for Jenny to attend to at the EGO compound. The disappearance of the leader of the company, and such a world-famous presence to boot, could only be concealed for so long.

Once news got out, the value of the company would plummet – and not only the technology company. If the panic spread to the cryptocurrency exchange he also personally ran, the value of Richstream might be affected even worse, potentially destroying the savings of millions of people around the world – a high price indeed, for a ploughman's lunch.

I explained all this discreetly to Holmes as Ms Yuen had the driver take us to the church. To my relief, Holmes did not make a big production of it. 'It's been there for eight hundred years, after all,' he said, after striding round and peering in through holes in the masonry. 'Just a worn-out relic, left over from a very different time. Like us, Watson!'

13

Before we left on the train back to Waterloo, Sherlock Holmes shook Jenny's hand and spoke reassuringly to her.

'Your commitment to Mr Glebe, and your concern about him, does you honour. If I can help resolve this matter I shall do so as fast and discreetly as possible.'

'You are kind,' she said, visibly touched by politesse.

Holmes bowed as the doors closed, and watched her as the train pulled away.

'That young woman is mightily impressive, but I've never seen someone so conflicted. I feel instinctively that she is an honest person. Yet, do you know, Watson, I think she hardly said a single true thing to us, all day!'

'Surely you're joking, Holmes?' I asked.

'As it happens, I am not,' he said stiffly. 'Did you take the chance to have a look at Mr Glebe's password? Pretty nifty handiwork that, I thought.'

'I looked closely,' I said. 'As far as I could make out, his password was "MEMORY".'

'Close,' said Holmes. 'There was no "e".'

I pondered. ' "Mammary"?'

'One might argue that would be in keeping with his rustic Australian sense of humour – but still not quite. Oh, you are missing your favourite drink, Watson. Fancy a cup? I shall go off and get one from the buffet car.'

I awoke some time later. The first thing I noticed was that the train had stopped. And when I opened my eyes, the lights went out.

'Goodness, Holmes! What is happening?'

'Remain calm, Watson. The train has stopped in a tunnel. I'm sure the lights will be back on in a moment.'

There was a crackle over the tannoy and a voice apologized for the delay.

'I'm sorry to inform you,' said the driver, 'that South West Rail has been the victim of a ransomware attack. All control of the service has been temporarily suspended. Erm – this is a new one on me, folks, but I'll give you more news when I get it . . .'

'This is ridiculous!' said Holmes. 'We could be here for weeks . . .'

'Holmes,' I said quietly. Our eyes were starting to adjust to the dimness, and we became aware that there was a third person sitting with us in the gloom. A hunched, nervous-looking figure.

'Are you Sherlock Holmes?' it asked.

'You have the advantage of me, sir!' said Holmes, grabbing his stick. 'Watson – your revolver!'

'There's no need for that, please – I assure you!' said the man. 'My name is Geoffrey Braithwaite. When I saw you get on the train at Tubmouth I was hoping to have a chance to speak to you. Mr Holmes . . . I assume you were there to investigate Igor Glebe?'

'I'm not in the habit of discussing the private matters of my clients,' said Holmes, still keeping his stick handy in case the man came closer.

' "Clients"? You cannot be working *for* this monster?'

'Mr Braithwaite!' said Holmes. 'This is a most irregular interview . . . I do not—'

'I *beg* you to listen,' Braithwaite said, sounding more nervous than ever. 'It is of the most crucial importance. Certainly to me – and, I am convinced, to many others as well! I am at my wits' end!'

These were words ideally chosen to smite the heart of Sherlock Holmes. Although he was only visible to me in outline, I saw his manner change as his intellect quickened.

'Fear not,' Holmes said. 'I have wits enough for the three of us. Pray go on.'

'I am an investigative journalist,' said Braithwaite. 'I've been investigating EGO for some time. There are many serious accusations against them – and Glebe personally. Breaches of medical and ethical rules. Brain experiments done in the development of this new device of theirs.'

'Brain experiments?' said Holmes.

'Yes. Conducted on a small Pacific island where there's next to no governmental oversight – San Colombo, it's called. From what I've been able to find out, the results were astonishing, but lots of subjects died. And it was all covered up. Because it means billions to them – potentially hundreds of billions. So they'll do anything to stop the truth getting out.'

'Such as?' Holmes asked.

'I went today to pose some questions to Glebe himself, to give him a chance to go on the record in response to these accusations. After he received my request, multiple accusations against *me* arrived at my newspaper, just this morning. Accusations that I faked stories, invented sources, on dozens of occasions.'

'You can deny these . . .' said Holmes.

'It was a fait accompli,' said Braithwaite. 'A dossier of fabrications, which would take months if not years to look into. Brilliantly forged and faked. Within an hour of my editor's receiving it, I was fired. I'll lose everything. My wife is desperately ill and I'm afraid I'll lose her as well . . .'

'But there are recourses, surely . . .' said Holmes.

Braithwaite emphatically shook his head. 'You don't understand. There were four of us journalists looking into EGO. Convinced there was a story there. All working at different papers. The "Gang of Four", we were nicknamed. One was in a car crash on holiday in Greece last summer, and is in a coma. The second just disappeared – completely vanished one night, just after Christmas. The third suddenly quit his job six weeks ago and won't answer anyone's calls or messages. I was the only one left.'

'What can I do about this?' asked Holmes.

'Watch your step,' said Braithwaite. 'This man has a gigantic amount of power and no hesitation about using it. He is a merciless psychopath with limitless access to surveillance. I cannot continue this fight. But if you do . . .' He leant in and whispered earnestly:

'Be careful, be cautious, but most important of all, *be Sherlock Holmes.*'

'My eyesight is perfect, Watson. I can easily make out that
dog over there, for instance.'

An electric crackle made us jump.

'Ladies and gentlemen,' said the driver's voice. 'I'm pleased to announce that the ransom appears to have been paid with impressive speed, and the energy switched back on. I'm looking at a green light here and we should be moving shortly. Sincere apologies for the delay to your service today!'

'Mr Braithwaite, what shall y—' I began.

But he was gone.

'Well, well, Watson,' said Holmes quietly, as the carriage made its first shunt forwards out of the tunnel. 'The friendly, funny, kind, pub-loving football fan who is also a merciless billionaire psychopath. What do you make of that?'

I simply shook my head in wonderment. Too many thoughts rushed in at once for me to be able to give voice to any of them.

Holmes and I remained in thoughtful silence for the rest of our journey, and getting out at Waterloo, queued patiently at the gate and meandered with the crowd onto the concourse, where we turned to each other to discuss our next movements.

We both opened our mouths – and then looked around, distracted.

'Yes, you,' said a deep, smooth voice.

I looked over my shoulder, and Holmes swivelled to look behind him.

'Cooo-eeeee,' said the voice. It was loud, and seemed to come from all around us. I realized it had an Australian accent, and the hairs on the back of my neck began to prickle uncomfortably. 'Up here!'

We both looked up.

At some recent time a gigantic screen had been erected above the concourse, perhaps a hundred feet across. I had never paid attention to it before, except for my eyes to glide over the silent advertisements playing on it. Now it showed the eyes of a face I recognized.

'Mr Holmes,' said the voice, 'and look, Dr Watson too. I've got one thing to say to you: *boo!*'

He chuckled. I looked at Holmes in disbelief – he was transfixed. I glanced around, and found that no one else was paying the slightest attention to this new variation in the accustomed and relentless noise of a major London terminus.

'Thanks for taking part in my little game today,' said Glebe playfully. 'I have to admit I enjoyed setting you a little puzzle. Just another one of my "pranks", as you called them earlier. I hope you had fun – a nice day out in the country, I reckon, for one of your age! But I'm kinda busy, so the game's over. Have the afternoon off. Try a billionaire's shortbread maybe. G'day, mate!'

He winked. And was gone.

The screen was filled by glossy footage of a four-by-four driving along an exotic beach, beside a galloping horse. The speakers broke back in to advise on the late running of the Guildford via Cobham service.

I put my hand on Holmes's shoulder for support.

'Did you notice what I did, Watson?' asked Holmes.

I begged him to tell me.

'He could hear everything we said to Jenny Yuen, in all our private conversations with her today. And not a single other person in this entire station paid any attention to what just happened.'

16

Holmes was right. People rushed along, talking on their phones or glancing up at the train times. Nobody seemed to have noticed anything amiss. 'How is it possible?' I asked.

'I daresay a few dozen people glanced up at the screen momentarily, but just dismissed it as some sort of advertisement they don't have time for,' said Holmes. 'In a place so overwhelmed with sound pollution as Waterloo station, people have learned to pay attention only to what they have to.'

'But that's shocking,' I said. I kept looking – determined to spot one confused soul, but failing.

'I wonder if Mr Glebe wants us to be shocked,' said Holmes grimly. 'By the realization that when we think we are alone, we can be listened in on – and when we think we are safe in public, we can be quite alone . . .'

On our return to Baker Street, Mrs Hudson met us at the front door.

'Mr Holmes, there is a nice young person waiting for you in your rooms. She seems most unhappy about something. I'll make some tea – ah, I see you got my text about buying some nice biscuits . . .' she said, taking the billionaire's shortbread I handed to her.

Holmes stopped just outside the door to our rooms. He took a deep breath, and let it out slowly. Then, opening the door (and before he could see who was within), he said graciously: 'Ms Yuen, I was sincerely hoping you would visit us!'

'Mr Holmes!' said the charming young woman, sitting up in the chair reserved for visitors and looking like a rabbit in the headlights. 'How did you . . .'

'You must allow me to make a few little deductions here and there,' he said soothingly, sitting in his own customary place, opposite from her, beside the unlit fire. 'You have made quite remarkable time, however. Now, my dear – you will forgive me calling you "my dear", I hope – it's been a long and momentous day for us both. Mrs Hudson will be in with tea in a moment, as well as a little sarcastic snack, and Dr Watson will be good enough to open the window so I might vape. You don't mind? It's only allowed on special occasions for me, these days . . .'

Holmes could be difficult, rude and at times utterly impossible. But he had a peculiar sensitivity towards distressed women, and could be remarkably caring when he chose. At such moments one wondered whether Holmes might have led a fulfilling romantic life, but then, of course, there had only ever been one woman for him – *the* woman – and that was long ago.

His soothing manner and expert small talk brought about a calming effect on Jenny's nerves. (And all the while I knew he, too, was recovering from a series of surprises and performing any number of shrewd mental gymnastics.)

Once we were all caffeinated, and reposing in the nicotine-tinctured scent of rose petals from Holmes's meerschaum vape, he allowed Jenny Yuen to give the reason for her visit.

'I just wanted to apologize for acting so foolishly today,' she said.

'I don't acknowledge the charge,' said Holmes sternly. 'You were kind, helpful and most informative.'

'Um, well – you know . . . I suppose "be that as it may" is what you would say in my place. The whole thing was a hoax. I found out later. It's so embarrassing. Mr Glebe wants you to desist the inquiry at once.'

'Does he *really*?' asked Holmes – and at the same time he shot out a hand to rest on my arm, to forestall any unhelpful interdiction I might make. 'I find that most surprising. He's turned up alive and well, then?'

'He has, yes. It was a joke that he never meant to get out of hand – and then an issue came up with the new product in the middle of the night, and he clean forgot all about you. When he's problem-solving he forgets everything and everyone. He's like that. Brilliant, but scatter-brained, as I said. Um, and I felt I had to say it to you directly. Only polite, after all your efforts.'

'I shall honour his wishes, of course. You are most kind to make this trip in person. Have another square of the shortbread. Or don't. Revolting, isn't it. I have only two small questions I would love you to answer, and then you have my word you shall never hear from me again.'

This last promise made such a positive improvement in Ms Yuen's mood that her face cleared of the anxiety which had been plainly written on it from the start of the interview. She agreed at once.

'First, have you ever seen Mr Kostak's security building

so densely populated? There was hardly enough space for anyone to sit down this morning.'

'No,' she said carelessly. 'I'm not often in there, but I have been in a handful of times. There's usually about ten staff, I'd say. I suppose they had a lot to check after the storm . . .'

'And second, what jobs will you be applying for tomorrow?'

'Holmes!' I said.

He looked askance at me, as Jenny Yuen's face drained of colour. 'A perfectly reasonable question, Watson,' he said. 'A very successful young professional like our friend here does not let the grass grow under her feet. She tendered her resignation at about two o'clock this afternoon. Is that not right?'

Jenny gulped, and nodded. I gazed at her.

'I don't know what I want to do next,' she said, avoiding our eyes. 'A change of sector maybe. It's been very intense, working at EGO. I need a new challenge. But to pay the bills I'll do something simple, maybe bar work in Tubmouth, we'll see . . .'

'You answered my questions, and a deal is a deal. I wish you well, young woman.'

She smiled uncertainly – and, thanking us, left.

As the door closed and we heard her footsteps on the stairs, Holmes relaxed in his chair.

'She does not know that Mr Glebe appeared to us at Waterloo station, and instructed us to cease our inquiries,' said Holmes quietly. 'Which suggests to me one of two things. Either she made this visit to Baker Street entirely of her own accord, without Mr Glebe's knowledge – and why would she do that? *Or*, that was not Mr Glebe who spoke to us at Waterloo. Interesting, don't you think?'

'Most!' I agreed. 'What do you make of it?'

'Well, there are two mysteries, Watson,' he said, settling back in his chair and closing his eyes. 'First: what happened? That's easy enough. But also: why? And "why" is equal to "what will happen next"? There's a real mystery, eh?'

'Eh?' I asked. 'I mean, is it? Is there?'

But the only response I received was a mellow snore from the corner of his armchair. Retrieving the great man's vape and propping his feet on a footstool, I left him to sleep.

17

I attended to some small matters at my desk for a while. So many of the cases I investigated with Holmes arrived in such a jumble or a heap of confusing events that I was almost accustomed to the sensation of complete bewilderment which now overtook my thinking brain.

There was Glebe's disappearance, the unfortunate fate of Braithwaite and his dire warnings, the inexplicable resignation of the formerly committed Ms Yuen, and finally Glebe's reappearance and closing of the case. I could make nothing of it.

Then, of course, there was the fact that Holmes had promised not to pursue the case, and was undoubtedly a man of his word. It was over.

Yet there were so many intriguing details, and so many unanswered questions, my mind kept going back to them and I yearned for the moment of explanation. For merely human minds like my own, it is best to busy oneself with mundane tasks and the comforting rhythm of ordinariness – and wait for the next development. It would come when Holmes had settled all the details to his satisfaction and tied up the loose threads, and decided it was time to tell me.

I could not help but notice that his behaviour was growing ever more erratic and unpredictable these days – and not with the illuminating lightning-flashes of old.

Now it was forgotten passwords, and uncertainty as to day or month.

Suddenly he was awake from his snooze and putting on his coat.

I could not quite put my finger on it, but something about his appearance told me that Holmes had been out whale hunting again.

'I am going out,' said Holmes. 'For some "fresh air", as we euphemistically describe the fumes of this sweltering metropolis, and to clear my head after a most confusing day . . .'

I wished him well and continued working for a few hours until, happening to come out of our rooms, I spied Holmes on the stairs.

'A refreshing walk, Holmes?' I asked.

'What?' he said.

'You're coming in, I assume?'

'What's that?' he said, irritably. 'Oh, don't plague me with questions.' And he marched past me back into our receiving room. I looked down at the stairs where he had been standing, apparently unsure whether he was going up or down.

'Shepherd's pie for dinner,' I said merrily, 'as it's a Wednesday. I, for one, am famished after all that racing about.'

Holmes was standing, looking at the empty fireplace.

'Holmes?' I asked.

'Hmm? Yes?'

'You must be hungry.'

He snapped out of his reverie and fixed me with a smile. 'Pardon me, Watson, I *am* scatty these days – I think a walk is in order. Clear my head.' And so saying, he turned and went out at once.

I watched the space where he had been standing. Despite the August warmth, I suddenly felt a chill.

18

'I saw another one of those "artworks" that look like computer drawings,' he said over dinner the next evening. 'In a street behind Euston station.'

'It seems the newspapers have dubbed the artist "Bitsy",' I said.

'Indeed,' said Holmes.

'And Mr Glebe has been active. Several news stories about his latest wild statements today. He's back with a vengeance!'

'Hmm?' said Holmes.

I repeated myself, but he showed no sign of listening.

The next day I came back from an appointment to discover Sherlock Holmes lolling (I can think of no other word) on the sofa in his dressing gown. The television was on, which was practically a gala event in itself. The device had been purchased to watch the coronation, and except for during the King's Christmas speech, it simply gathered dust.

'What is this programme, Holmes?' I said peering at the screen. On it, teenagers were bickering about some small emotional matter.

'Shhhh,' he said, waving me away. Then I saw, of all things, an open pizza box beside him.

I retreated to my desk, but the noise of the set was too interfering, so I gathered some papers and made my way to my own room to pursue my work.

I ought to have been happy to see Holmes relaxing like this – I had often enough begged him to take some time off, and to learn how to unwind. But despite myself, I was unsettled by the sight.

After I had been working a while I tiptoed to my door and opened it a crack.

Holmes was still watching the screen, agog. In one hand was a seemingly forgotten slice of pizza. As before, a rather petulant disagreement was in progress on the screen. I noticed now the participants were talking in Australian accents.

'Omigod,' murmured Holmes. 'Wait till Helen Daniels hears about *that* . . .' He let out a pizza burp.

As the episode ended, a sentimental tune helpfully instructed me that neighbours should be there for one another.

I closed the door as quietly as I could, and retreated.

19

There was much to consume me in the late-summer weeks that followed.

I had recently discovered that online there were a multitude of products being sold on their apparent likeness to myself and Holmes. There was a search engine, Ask Sherlock, which appeared to have been going for twenty years.

Someone with the name Dr John Watson had opened a cosmetic surgery business in St John's Wood, advertising his wares with a model wearing nothing but a bikini and a deerstalker hat.

A drinks company in Bulgaria had produced an 'energy drink' with most decidedly unhealthy ingredients, called W.M.D. – Watson's Medicinal Distillation. It featured an illustration of a leering snake-oil salesman with a top hat and stethoscope, which with deep affront I took to be myself.

Addressing these fake alternate selves, which had sprung up seemingly everywhere, became all of a sudden my primary concern.

As time went on I became embroiled in a war of legal letters that was as expensive as it was dispiriting. I felt like someone who finds himself in quicksand, where every attempt to free myself dragged me deeper into trouble. I was soon overwhelmed.

Holmes was no help.

He had been no stranger to fits of inactivity over the years, but the one that had hold of him at present was of a different character entirely. Where he had used to seem furiously distracted by his own internal complexities, now his habitual expression was glassy and torpid.

Defying all logic, he appeared to have become addicted to two Australian soap operas: *Neighbours* and *Home and Away*. He watched episodes back to back for days on end, lying in a lethargic semi-snooze upon the ottoman.

In the meantime, I could not help occasionally catching references to the infamous Igor Glebe. It seemed to be the unanimous conclusion of all the world's media that he was Good Copy. Wherever one turned there was coverage of his public spats, his cosying up to right-wing ideologues, his casual ableism: the Glebe charm offensive proceeded without slowing.

Speculation about the specific capabilities and release date of the NEXT-GEN device became ever more fervent. For some reason the excitement drowned out completely any doubts about the medical provenance of the device – I heard no mention of the illegal experiments, the supposed victims, or the island of San Colombo.

If there was any truth to those rumours, then Glebe's success in getting away with it and escaping censure – indeed, soaring ever upwards in wealth and fame – was a hideous possibility, a dark blot on my thoughts.

My mind turned to poor Mr Braithwaite, and how he might be faring. What had he said? 'Most important of all, *be Sherlock Holmes.*' Not for the first time recently, I experienced a twinge of doubt, and cast a look at my friend where he sat on the sofa.

But Holmes showed no interest in anything nowadays except daytime Australian television dramas.

Requests for new cases arrived, and he ignored them.

All zest for detection appeared to have abandoned him.

A lacuna, or a hiatus, had arisen in our affairs. I began to entertain thoughts of leaving Holmes, to return to my country retreat and take up my retirement full-time. Nothing lasts forever, after all, and all things have their seasons.

Holmes and I had had a better run than many other partnerships. We had undoubtedly had some thrilling times and magnificent triumphs.

That I contemplated my next step with mixed feelings would be a cruel understatement. Yet, feeling disloyal as I did so, I began to make plans to move on.

And then, one Tuesday afternoon, Mrs Hudson called me downstairs. She looked most upset.

'My dear Mrs H!' I said. 'What is it?'

'The police,' she said.

Vicky Lestrade stood at the front door, looking grave.

'I'm sorry, Dr Watson,' she said. 'It's not good.'

20

Lestrade drove me to the hospital, and on the way explained what had happened.

'He was found wandering in Hyde Park,' she said. 'He seemed confused and upset, and when a police officer offered to help, became abusive.'

'Oh dear,' I said, for the twentieth time. 'Oh dear, oh dear.'

'He broke the young PC's nose,' said Vicky. 'There's a chance that we might be able to persuade the officer not to press charges, considering the great services you have provided in the past.'

'Oh dear!' I said again. Apparently I could not think of anything else to say.

When she showed me to the ward where he was being kept, the great detective saw me and started out of his torpor. Some of his humour and colour returned.

'Ghastly misunderstanding, Watson!' he said. 'Thank god you're here. Can't get these devils to take the metal cuffs off me. Can you believe it!'

I took his hand in mine, and held it. I was horrified how thin his arms looked in the hospital gown.

'Watson, you look worried,' he said quietly, looking me over. 'Is something wrong? Has something happened?' His gaze was kindly and innocent, almost schoolboyish. It cut me to the quick.

'No, no,' I said, my throat suddenly tight. 'Let us go home.'

'Good old Watson,' he said. 'Can we watch *Home and Away*?'

'Of course we can,' I said. 'I'd love to.'

'Are you sure nothing's wrong, Watson?' – in the same considerate voice as before. 'You look like you could cry. Buck up there, my man!'

I tried to.

21

The next morning found me in the Harley Street surgery of Dr Muir Agar, who saw me at once owing to a favour Holmes had been able to provide him in the past.

'It can be more difficult for men like Holmes,' he said, 'who are used to absolute command of their faculties. It can be a great struggle to adapt to this new reality. He will have peaks and troughs – times when he's almost back to his old self. He is very lucky to have such a friend as you, Dr Watson.'

How my conscience smote me at these words! To think I had been so recently contemplating leaving Holmes and moving off on my own . . .

Dr Agar gave me all the helpful advice he could – supplying me with literature, resources, telephone numbers and much more.

At Baker Street, we settled into a steady routine. Holmes began his afternoon walks again, but now I elected to walk with him, insisting that I also needed some fresh air. He watched his TV programmes while I worked quietly on my legal affairs – and these modest memoirs of my life with him, which were for me at that time a precious distraction.

Holmes inhabited a shadowland, a kind of continuous daze interrupted only on one occasion when I thought I heard his old, knowing chuckle – a genuinely mirthful sound. I looked up to see a report on Igor Glebe on the television screen. I could have sworn that for a moment I had heard Holmes mutter: 'Hogwash!'

'Holmes?' I asked. 'Did you speak?' He met my eye and for one moment I saw the familiar intelligent gleam. But it was fleeting, and gone so fast I thought I'd imagined it.

He'd already switched the channel and was lost among the denizens of Erinsborough.

'I believe you meant "you're", not "your",'
Holmes patiently explained.

Another week passed before Holmes next seemed to rally.

It happened suddenly. In the middle of an episode of *Neighbours*, he sat up straight and switched off the television. There was something different in his demeanour – upright and purposeful as of old, like a hound on the scent. He looked around the room for a few moments before his eye settled on me.

'Watson,' he said thoughtfully. 'Let's go to a football match.'

It was a request that was quite as uncharacteristic as his recent televisual habits. But I could not consider denying him this, so I immediately began to investigate games to go to. I might as well not have bothered – of course, Holmes already knew which match he wanted to see.

Therefore, the following afternoon found us in a group of about seventy people by the touchline of a hummocky, balding pitch as twenty-two men jogged on. We were here to watch Tubmouth & Crettingdean FC (already languishing at eighteenth in the Hobson's Building Supplies League Southwest, only three games into the season) against the Densbury Owls (hovering respectably at fifth).

Holmes blew on the steaming cup of tea he held in his hand, and looked at the other supporters. I offered to fetch him a pie, but at that moment the whistle blew, and Holmes pointed out that as the stand was run by the

Tubmouth goalkeeper we would have to wait until half-time for further refreshment.

'Paul Brann, the "Burger Meister", as the sign proclaims him,' Holmes explained, 'has to fill in in goal this week, because last week at Gillhurst the goal fell over and the crossbar hit the regular keeper, Jim Clarke. He's off until November with two detached retinas.'

'You appear to be up to speed on the goings-on at Tubmouth & Crettingdean, Holmes,' I observed.

'I've glanced in the newspaper now and then to follow them since we found out that Mr Glebe bought the club. You saw the picture on the clubhouse wall?'

I had – it showed the grinning Australian handing over a gigantic cardboard cheque while shaking hands with the club's chairwoman, who was also the local undertaker.

The game itself was a stop-start affair. Densbury gave a spirited early series of attacks, which Tubmouth repulsed with a defensive technique that was lumpy and lacking grace, but stubbornly effective.

'That's Dumughn, the left back,' Holmes said into my ear. 'Wouldn't want to meet him down a dark alley, eh, Watson? Absolute piledriver of a left foot, too.'

Standing on the touchline provided a surprisingly sensory experience: there was more audible squelching from the boots and wheezing from the players than I had anticipated. And at one point, when a clearance came towards the crowd, it was headed back on by a bald fellow, which was rewarded by a cheer and some polite clapping. The teams, however, were in deadlock, and half-time arrived with no score.

In the second half, with the crowd's hunger sated by

fresh pies (or, rather, freshly consumed stale pies), the entertainment level suddenly rose. Dumughn sent out a long clearance; a Densbury player skidded and fell over in the mud; midfielder Danny Solomon met the clearance and sprinted into space . . .

The crowd roared: we all spotted the Densbury keeper out of his area, picking up a child's kite that had fallen on the pitch. Solomon lofted it in with ease from thirty yards, and as he pulled his shirt over his head in celebration, it tore in half, leaving it flapping.

'The game's afoot, Watson!' cried Holmes.

23

Six minutes later, Densbury equalized from the penalty spot. They seemed likely to take the lead when their right winger, accelerating to meet a crafty cross-pitch pass, collided with the door of a Ford Cortina that had just parked on the edge of the penalty area, and knocked himself out.

An elderly lady climbed from the car with her yapping dog and got into a lengthy shouting match with the Densbury team, until the referee showed her a red card for the third time, at which she drove off in a spray of mud.

By this point the home crowd was in decidedly high spirits. A last-minute tap-in from the new Tubmouth attacker, a dark and handsome Ukrainian refugee named Leon Dyskov, secured three points and was the cherry on the cake.

'Watson!' Holmes carolled to me. 'Why did you never tell me football was this amusing? I feel I've been missing out all these years!'

'Holmes, it does me good to see you so lively,' I said, as the crowd started to disperse around us. 'I never guessed you would develop a sudden taste for association football!'

'Do not be deceived, Watson – I am not *particularly* fond of soccer. I *am* here, however, to speak to Mr Morris Jayne! How do you do, sir?'

At these words a man a few yards away spun round. He was ruddy-faced, portly and about sixty years of age, with bulging eyes which swivelled left and right, looking for who had called his name. Sherlock Holmes took a step forward and took his hand.

Mr Jayne was a little startled, but still under the charm or glamour of victory, and delighted to talk to a fellow fan. (The away fans – a woman and a child – were drifting away from the opposite touchline.)

I watched as Holmes attempted to keep up with Jayne's commentary on the performance of Tubmouth & Crettingdean.

'Yes, yes,' Holmes agreed, 'it *is* a very slow pitch after heavy rain. It was indeed a wise stratagem to play a steady defensive game and use conserved energy to make some daring late attacks. I quite agree. Now, sir – my name is Holmes. You received my letter, I think?'

This at last stopped Mr Jayne's enthusiastic flow. He looked stunned for a moment and then clapped his hand to his forehead. 'Of course!' he said. 'How stupid of me! I was wondering how you . . . Here . . . I've got it here . . .'

He reached into an inside pocket and produced a thick brown envelope, which he handed over. Holmes thanked him sincerely, while Jayne immediately turned to another fan of his acquaintance, and his discussion of the game continued.

'Not taking bungs on the touchline, Holmes?' I asked.

He chuckled and patted the packet with satisfaction, before placing it under his arm. 'Not exactly. This could be very important indeed. Let's make sure we keep it safe, Watson. It should be the proof we've been looking for!'

'Proof?' I said. 'Of what?'

'Well,' Holmes said, taking my arm in his as we walked

from the field, 'I don't mind telling you that Mr Jayne over there has the largest collection of VHS cassettes in the British Isles. Including . . . a very rare missing episode of *Neighbours*, from 2003!'

I had allowed myself to feel the first faint stirring of hope that the old Holmes was back. At least for a while. That hope now began to fade.

'Holmes,' I said. 'I believe I shall never understand you, as long as I live.'

'Not long now, Watson,' he said quietly. 'Not long, and you'll understand all.'

When in need of distraction, Sherlock Holmes relaxed with a few rounds of 'indoor tennis golf', a game of his own creation.

24

The joy of an afternoon with Holmes on good form gave me sustenance. But its glow dissipated as I noticed he said barely a few words on the whole railway journey home.

From that moment, I noticed the old Sherlock starting to vanish. His comment that all would be revealed was, I knew, empty bravado – he had already forgotten it.

There was little to enjoy in the dark days that followed. Baker Street was a sombre place. Some kind visitors (Lestrade Sr and Jr) came more frequently. Others, afraid of their own emotions perhaps, or of having some deleterious effect on the Great Man, stayed away.

Mrs Hudson, who worshipped Holmes, was never to be seen without eyes that were red and puffy – but that wonderful woman neglected not one of her duties in the smallest regard.

Soon pieces appeared in the popular press commenting on the supposed 'disappearance' of Sherlock Holmes. No doubt the online world, if I had chosen to access it, was speculating with as much heartless flippancy as Fleet Street.

I learned that Sherlock had been killed; kidnapped by

Russian agents; brainwashed; replaced with a sentient AI, or indeed a robot . . .

At last, disaster struck. A journalist put two and two together, and rustled up an unnamed source from Dr Agar's office.

The news was out.

'I am most dreadfully sorry,' Dr Agar said to me the following day, when I visited him. 'It is a monstrous breach of privacy . . . If there's anything I can do . . .'

'I just care about Holmes,' I said. 'What can be done? There are journalists outside Baker Street with telephoto lenses, round the clock. The intrusion – and think what might they see . . .'

'There, I think I can help,' Agar replied, and his reassuring doctorly manner took possession of him again. 'I know a place perfect for just this occasion. It's not easy to get admittance – but I can pull a few strings . . .'

He reached for the phone.

25

Agar was as good as his word.

That evening, Holmes and myself were whisked by private car with dark windows to the front doors of a sleek black skyscraper. We were admitted by a uniformed footman and taken to the thirtieth floor, and thence into what could only be described as a secretive and luxurious palace of healthcare.

'This is the only facility of its kind in the world,' said the soft-spoken nurse who had been assigned to us. 'It offers absolute and complete security from outside intrusion. It was constructed specially for this purpose: the very walls and windows are lined with military-grade materials equivalent to those in a nuclear bunker. They do not allow signals of any kind – telephone, radar, anything you can think of. If you wish to speak to me, you pull on this bell – it operates via a rope, as in an old country house – and I'll hear it in the next room. You are *absolutely safe* from any intrusion or interference from the outside world.'

She left us to look along the plush corridors and explore the games room, where board games and billiards were being played quietly by other residents. Discovering on a wall map that there was a pool on the top floor, I decided a paddle might be a pleasing distraction.

A few minutes later we were in the deserted pool area;

the underlit waves reflected attractively from the glass ceiling, while a handful of stars glinted above in the night sky over London.

'How do you like this, my dear fellow?' I asked, as we approached the pool. 'Whoever thought such a thing existed?'

'I did,' said Holmes quietly.

'Oh, you did?' I said. 'It shouldn't surprise me. I wouldn't put anything past a clever old stick such as—'

'Don't patronize me, Watson,' he said evenly. 'Naturally I engineered it that we should end up here. So that, free from surveillance, we might speak properly for the first time in weeks.'

I stepped back and regarded him, twin emotions rising in me.

'Holmes?' I asked.

'It is I, Watson.'

'Holmes!'

'Watson – can you ever forgive me for what I've put you through?'

I pushed him in.

26

He looked stupefied for a second and, trying to turn in mid-air, hit the water face first with an almighty splash that I am humble enough to admit I found satisfying.

'Touché,' he said, spitting water from his mouth when he surfaced. 'I deserved that.'

I held out a towel for him while he clambered from the water.

'I have so many questions,' I said.

'Of course you must. Let us talk – time is precious. Unless I am much mistaken, all will be revealed *very soon.*'

'What is this about? What case can you have been on?'

'Igor Glebe, of course!' he said, throwing the towel around his shoulders. 'That monstrous company EGO, and their murderous cover-ups.'

'Why all this . . . all this deception? And how do you mean to catch Glebe?'

'Let us sit, and I'll explain,' he said, starting to dry himself. 'It was obvious from the moment that apparition spoke to us at Waterloo station – and also from what Braithwaite had told us on the train – that there was something terrible going on, and that we had no privacy. Also, look at Jenny Yuen, who loved Glebe *the man*, but hated Glebe the public entity. She came to Baker Street to tell us not to investigate, visibly frightened, not knowing her boss had already contacted us. She was trying to *protect* us from what might happen if we looked into things. So, as I say: it was very obvious that something very bad was happening, and that it was next to impossible to investigate under such circumstances. Every word we spoke to each other, *everywhere*, was overheard. I had to make myself appear as unthreatening as possible, or risk being silenced like the others. How wonderful it is to be able to speak normally again!'

I nodded. 'Glebe wanted us to know it – to back off. To be afraid.'

'Well, not really. You see, Igor Glebe does not exist.'

'It is a case of murder?' I ran through the facts I knew, and could not square this conclusion with them.

'Not at all. You see, this has always been *two* cases. The first I solved before we left Tubmouth station that day. Igor Glebe has never existed. He was an actor, hired by some malevolent entity who needed to remain secret. I expect he was told it would be a once-in-a-lifetime part, a brilliant and demanding performance that would make him famous and boost his career. Once he was in, of course – it was too late. He could not escape.'

'Except he *did* escape!' I said.

'Exactly. He started making impromptu excursions from the EGO compound. He was desperate to experience a bit of normal life. On one of those, at the Dog and Star pub – a woman bumped into him. I am convinced she gave him the means to escape permanently.'

'How did you know that had happened?' I marvelled.

'I didn't – I merely mentioned to the barmaid that *something* unexpected had occurred, and she filled in the rest.

I already knew it was a breakout – did you notice how similar the EGO headquarters were to a prison? Ms Yuen more or less said so herself. And the tree – remember how I sat on the stump to clean my boots? It was so that she would not see the tree had been *deliberately* felled. Remember how a tree that has blown down in a storm looks? It's an explosion of giant splinters. This had been cut down with an axe.'

'Brilliant!'

'And I know who did it. Recall how your shirtsleeve was covered with paint, where you had brushed against the EGO compound outer wall?'

'Yes,' I said. 'I cursed my bad luck – and their quickness at repainting their wall!'

'But you did not see what your lucky accident exposed beneath the paint, Watson. A distinct part of a QR code! A message from Glebe's partner in crime to the powers at EGO.'

My head spun. 'You mean . . .'

He nodded. 'The person who bumped against him in the pub, and helped him escape, is also the artist known as Bitsy – the mysterious individual who has been giving away millions for no known reason. We now know she is a woman and has a personal grudge against EGO, and against the person – who is definitely not Igor Glebe – behind the whole enterprise!'

'But Glebe has been a constant presence since his disappearance,' I protested. 'He's been in the news more than ever!'

'Never in person. His social media accounts have been active, yes, and he has posted video recordings of himself.

All fakes, easily produced by the real technological genius behind the scenes . . .'

'Amazing,' said a wondering voice. 'You really are amazing . . .'

Holmes and I had been absolutely convinced we were alone. Our heads swivelled and, at the far end, hidden in the shadows, we saw a familiar shape.

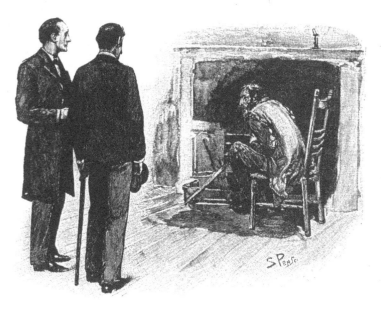

'When you said he looked like a wanker, Watson, I did
not realize you were being so literal.'

27

For a moment, Sherlock Holmes was lost for words. But only for a moment.

'Mr Braithwaite,' he said. 'Must you always be cloaked in shadow? Step forward, man, so we can see you!'

The journalist did. He looked older and smaller than when we had last seen him – but then we had not really seen him, even then.

'Mr Holmes, you've done everything I hoped for, and more,' he said. 'You are a marvel – a consummate genius . . .'

'Watson,' said Holmes, 'your revolver!'

'Don't be preposterous, Holmes, you know full well I don't have my revolver on me!'

'Well, dip that towel in the pool then – a wet towel will just about serve as a weapon!'

Braithwaite stopped. His joy at seeing us, which had for a moment sounded threatening to our ears, turned to confusion. 'What do you mean? You are joking, surely!'

'Am I?' said Holmes. He relaxed slightly. 'Well, perhaps I am, at that. Mr Braithwaite – you heard my explication of the case of Igor Glebe?'

'I did! And I am stunned! I've been continuing my investigations too, you see . . . I'm close, I can feel it. But my final proof is lacking . . .'

Now Holmes positively came off his guard. 'Thank

goodness. For a moment I thought I was going to have to drown you in this swimming pool. I am sincerely relieved it is not necessary.'

Again, confusion clouded Braithwaite's expression. 'You do have an odd sense of humour, Mr Holmes,' he said.

For some reason, I began to feel an unwelcome and familiar sensation in the hairs on the back of my neck.

'I don't believe in coincidences, you see,' said Holmes. 'Certainly not ones of this magnitude.'

Braithwaite's confusion teetered over into irritation. 'What are you talking about? You asked me to come here and meet you! You even organized my admittance here at the hospital!'

'MR HOLMES,' said a metallic voice. 'SHERLOCK HOLMES. PAY ATTENTION.'

28

The sound came from near the door. It was electronic and distorted.

'It's not possible,' said Braithwaite. 'No signal can get into or out of here! It's physically impossible!'

'It's a recording,' said Holmes. He cautiously approached the door and flicked the lights to their brightest. Nearby, under a cushioned wall seat, was a cupboard.

'YOU MUST OBEY THESE INSTRUCTIONS,' said the voice. 'YOU ARE TO LEAVE HERE AND GO TO THE NEXT STREET. GO TO THE FIRST FLOOR OF THE BOOKSHOP.'

Holmes reached out a foot and flicked the cupboard open with his toe. It was empty except for a Dictaphone, pushed right to the back.

'GO TO THE FICTION SECTION,' said the voice. 'APPROACH THE LOS ANGELES OLYMPICS. THEN LOOK OUT. YOU WILL KNOW WHAT TO DO.'

The recording stopped.

Holmes turned the Dictaphone over in his hand, as though frustrated that such a flimsy thing could have so much power over us.

'We'd better do it,' he said.

'Are you sure, Holmes?' I asked. 'It might be dangerous!'

'Oh, I don't think so,' said Holmes. He looked up at us

and smiled. That gleam, that self-satisfied air I knew so well, was back. My heart filled with the old excitement.

'Holmes,' I asked, 'might the game be afoot?'

We went to our separate apartments, dressed, and then repaired to the street. I admit to some trepidation that we might not be allowed to leave the hospital at such a late hour, but we received no breath of an objection.

The London streets were eerily quiet, a silence only broken by the occasional swish of a taxi as it sped on a crosswise street far behind or ahead.

The bookshop, when we found it, was still open, but as deserted as the streets. We made our way tentatively upstairs to Fiction, looking carefully all around us.

'What did he mean, "the Los Angeles Olympics"?' I asked. 'What the devil is going on?'

'After all this constant and oppressive surveillance we've been subjected to, Watson – you still fail to recognize a reference to Orwell?' Holmes plucked a copy of *Nineteen Eighty-Four* from the shelves and I dizzily recalled having once been aware that the Los Angeles Olympics had been in that year.

'Now, our instruction was to "look",' he said. We looked at each other, and then around again at the endless ranks of bookshelves – all perfectly empty of any person, or sign.

'Oh my god,' said Braithwaite suddenly. 'LOOK!' He ran to the window.

In the street below us stood a familiar figure, well-lit in the streetlight. The person who (according to Holmes) had until recently portrayed the character of Igor Glebe.

He smiled and waved to us. And then pointed.

On the wall of a house on the other side of the street was a giant QR code.

When we reached the level of the street, seconds later, the man was gone. Despite the fact that this man had been his obsession for many years, and the bane of his very existence, Geoffrey Braithwaite paid his disappearance no attention. Instead he was fumbling his phone out of his pocket and – fingers trembling – struggling to open the camera app.

He held the phone up. His nerves made it wobble violently, and he swore under his breath as the code failed to identify. Then it did. He clicked the link, letting out an enormous sigh of relief.

We all looked at what he saw. And then couldn't stop looking.

29

'What a disaster!' cried Holmes, from his familiar place by the fire at Baker Street. He closed his newspaper angrily.

'Holmes?' I asked.

'Both Dumughn and Ferguson are out for Tubmouth's next game, against the Shipminster Seagulls! Ferguson slipped a disc helping his neighbour move a piano, and Dumughn's tractor failed its MOT! What will we do?'

'Holmes,' I said. 'Slightly more pressing matters attend us. The next Braithwaite article just published! It's absolutely stunning!'

'You read it,' he said, opening his newspaper again. 'Then there's this. Our new manager's just moved from Lazio and doesn't speak a word of English. They've had to get a translator from a local pizza place. Listen. "Tubmouth manager Marcello Ribiani said in a statement: 'Tubmouth's performance is as spicy as the 'nduja on one of the delicious pizzas at Geraldo's Ristorante, 54 High Street, happy hour until seven, every day except Fri and Sat.'" How are we to achieve promotion under such farcical circumstances?'

I was too busy reading to respond.

On the night of our exciting meeting with Braithwaite we had effected an entrance to our Baker Street rooms in the small hours, eluding any journalists who might have been lurking.

Since then, Mr Braithwaite had not been idle. The cache of information which had downloaded to his phone contained damning details on a group of criminals, which he was busy turning into electrifying newsprint (or rather, news pixels).

Holmes noticed that PixieDreamGrl2001 looked slightly different from her profile picture.

It seemed that the mysterious Bitsy had had a precise plan all along. Every one of her stencilled artworks had been left on the wall of a building which belonged to a different criminal who was part of an underground network. The stencils exposed these individuals to public view, made their buildings noticeable and gave them the sort of unwelcome scrutiny they were at pains to avoid.

Braithwaite's pieces (for his old paper, which had welcomed him back with a front-page apology) were busy exploring this network – a kind of criminal exchange which communicated via a forum on the Dark Web.

'I must say, I am still *most* curious to know who this Bitsy person is,' said Holmes, finally folding up his newspaper. 'Partly of course so I can stop saying "Bitsy", a most irritating word. What is the latest Braithwaite news?'

This latest dispatch contained the most damning revelations of all. Braithwaite exposed that the total amount of cryptocurrency that Bitsy had stolen from these criminals and then given away added up to £13.8675 billion. And that EGO had in the past weeks urgently liquidated stock to that the same amount, almost to the crypto equivalent of a penny. The connection between EGO and the criminal network was obvious: the criminals were all EGO shareholders. Everyone around the world with an investment in Richstream (or 'Rch$trm', as its adherents preferred to write it) was busily divesting themselves of the currency. Its value (and that of EGO) was in freefall.

'Does it say the name of the Dark Web forum these criminals used, Watson?'

'I haven't finished reading it yet,' I said. 'By the sound of your voice, I'd say you have a fair idea what it is?'

'Indeed. Remember Mr Glebe's password? He deliberately typed it over and over, hoping that I would see that footage and understand. You remember I teased you about it?'

'Er, yes. I thought it was "memory", or – it had an "a" . . .'

'And I said you were forgetting your favourite drink, you recall?'

I did recall. 'Tea?' I said. I had never had the facility for anagrams that Holmes possessed – I tried to jumble the letters in my mind, but it was no good. I shook my head in bewilderment.

'I told you, didn't I, that there was something about the name "Richstream" which bothered me? Finally I realized. Now, Watson, you're much better at German than you are at anagrams. Tell me: what is a direct German translation of "Richstream"?'

I thought.

And a sudden horror dawned on me. 'No!' I said. 'It can't be! "Reichenbach"! And that means . . . Glebe's password was "MORIARTY"!'

'The very same,' said Holmes. 'I wonder if our old foe resented the fact that the Home Office Large Major Enquiry System is named after me? I say, Watson, this case is coming together nicely. Why don't we go outside and explain to the massed paparazzi that I'm right as rain again? And then, what say you to a steak dinner?'

30

'This has been two cases from the start,' said Holmes, as we walked along Baker Street minutes later, the journalists firmly dispersed by a few curt Holmesian sentences. 'We solved the first – the escape of the actor who was "playing" Igor Glebe. The second is much, *much* more momentous.'

He swung in to the Underground station at Baker Street and paid (as always and forever) by cash for a paper ticket.

'I've been led by the hand throughout, Watson,' he said, on the escalator. 'And have made hardly any deductions. I've been lagging behind all along.'

'Good lord,' I said, as we came onto the platform. 'I hadn't seen the time. Will there be any more trains at this hour?'

'I sincerely hope not!' said Holmes. The display told us the final service had indeed left. 'Duck in here,' he added, guiding me into a depression in the brickwork that was beyond the scope of the cameras.

'All shall be revealed,' he said quietly.

'How do you know?' I asked.

He pointed to a small inscription on the wall behind us. 'All shall be revealed,' it said, in tiny handwriting. At that moment all the lights in the station went off. Beneath where those words had been, written in luminescent ink, were the words: 'Look behind you.'

We both turned. On the wall opposite (in what was otherwise a total sea of darkness) was scrawled in tall capitals:

WELL HELLO, SHERLOCK

3 1

'Come on, Watson, it's quite safe. I assure you!' Holmes was attempting to cajole me down from the platform side to walk along the floor of the track. After our eyes had adjusted to the darkness, he walked along the narrow ledge that extended inside the tunnel's mouth, while I followed him uncertainly.

After fifty yards, there was an opening-out of the tunnel where lines crossed. Bright little arrows on the wall showed us where it was safe to walk. At the point where our path seemed most dangerous, one of them was addressed to me.

'DON'T WORRY WATSON!' it said.

'Now . . . here we go . . . this is more like it . . .' said Holmes, when we were deep within the tunnel and had been walking in darkness for some minutes. There were rumblings and distant reflected flashes of electric sparks, but we were never threatened by a direct oncoming train.

Holmes handed me up onto the platform of a long-abandoned station. It was ghostly, and still had advertisements on the walls for Bird's Custard and Capstan Cigarettes. A luminous arrow pointed towards a staircase, down from which came a shaft of light.

As we started up it, a woman's figure appeared above us.

'You got my invitation, then,' she said. 'Every good

detective reads the personal messages in *The Times*, of course, but this time I put one in the *Tubmouth Observer* as well, just to be sure.'

'A highly readable publication!' said Holmes. 'I don't miss an issue, these days.'

'"Tubby Cretins for ever"?' she said mockingly. 'I would never have expected it of you. Now – red or white?'

'With *steak*?' Holmes bellowed. 'Who do you think you are talking to? Red of course, Irene Adler!'

32

That the lithe silhouette at the top of the steps could by any stretch be Irene Adler, the only woman who Sherlock Holmes had ever truly admired, seemed to me impossible. She ought only to be a handful of years younger than Holmes and myself, and yet I found myself looking up at a youthful, athletic figure.

'Oh, do come on,' she said. 'I'm hungry.'

It was evident that she knew every secret passage and route through this underground warren – she led us at speed without ever having to stop or think.

'There is a city under the city,' she said. 'Much or most of it is abandoned. Or forgotten. For someone like me, who needs to be invisible, getting to know it has been invaluable. I've got a few spots where I can hang out in peace while the city buzzes above me. For now, though – let's go up here.'

She climbed up a metal ladder and waited for us to follow. I arrived at the top puffing, and then the three of us slipped from a dirty access door in the side of a brick arch, onto a cobbled street where revellers talked loudly, holding pint glasses and bottles.

'Wait,' she said. She handed each of us a mask. 'Put them on. Here – perfect. Now follow me . . .'

We stepped in through the side door of a bustling tavern to find ourselves in a crowd of people – who were all dressed like us. There were perhaps fifty Holmeses and not quite so many Watsons (although there were some costumes I struggled to identify), all enjoying themselves and talking loudly.

Irene Adler led us through the party and out onto the patio at the back of the pub, then stepped between late-night drinkers onto a floating restaurant. As Holmes and myself settled at the only table, taking off our masks (he had been wearing a Watson one, and I a Holmes), a waiter poured us each a glass of red wine. There was a swinging sensation as the boat left its mooring.

'Dinner on a private boat on the Thames,' Ms Adler said, sitting down with us. 'Only open to very special customers. Ernesto, the maître d' – a *darling* chap – and I are old friends. That whole Holmes-and-Watson-party thing was just to double, triple, *quadruple* check that we weren't being followed.'

'After all,' said Holmes, 'this *has* always been a case of stolen identities. You, if I may say so Ms Adler, appear entirely to have escaped the ravages of time.'

'Well, aren't you sweet. Actually, I have Dr Watson to thank for that,' she said.

I flushed, not knowing what she might mean, but she saw my discomfiture and laughed. 'That is, Dr John Watson, the talented cosmetic surgeon of St John's Wood. I was rather disappointed when I arrived that it did not turn out to be you, after all . . .'

'Which reminds me,' said Holmes, looking round for a waiter. 'I don't suppose you have any of that W.M.D. stuff? Watson's Medicinal Distillation? Marvellous drink . . .' The waiter frowned with incomprehension, and Holmes winked at me.

Adler lifted her glass and clinked it against Holmes's. Their eyes met.

I began to feel slightly like a third wheel. Or a spare rudder.

It was only after the tragedy that the authorities thought to put up a sign saying 'No Scottish Dancing Near Cliff Edge'.

33

'Time to explain things to Dr Watson,' Irene Adler said. 'How exciting! I've read your stories, of course, my dear doctor, with much pleasure. I've never been here for this bit.'

'Please,' I smiled. '"John" will be fine.'

'Look here, Watson,' said Holmes sternly. 'Are you "chatting up" my "bird"? You want a taste of the famous left jab?'

'Holmes!' I protested.

'Boys!' said Ms Adler. 'Keep it civil. We don't want anyone to have to be fished out half-drowned by the Thames River Police. We have much to discuss, and . . .' She checked her watch. 'A precise schedule to keep.'

'Indeed,' said Holmes. 'A case of stolen identities, assumed identities . . . I lost mine, Moriarty took one on, as did you, Irene. Igor Glebe never truly existed . . .'

'And there is one more,' she said. 'Will you tell Watson?'

'When the time comes,' Holmes said. 'But this has been your case all along. I've really been trailing behind you, feasting on what crumbs you threw my way. In fact, one of the only things I truly don't understand is, why did you involve me at all? I feel you could have done this all on your own . . .'

'*Typical* man,' she said. 'Thinks he's the centre of the

universe. I had no desire whatever for you to be on the case, Mr Holmes. That was our friend the actor's idea.'

'His name,' said Holmes, 'being James Clement.'

For the first time, Irene Adler looked surprised. 'How the devil do you know that? I had no intention of telling you.'

'Ah,' said Holmes. 'Well, feigning dementia as I had to, to protect both of our lives – for which I beg your forgiveness for the thousandth time, my very dear Watson – I had little else to do but sleuth his identity. A promising young Australian actor – and I hazarded a guess that he *was* truly Australian, as maintaining a fake accent round the clock for years on end must surely be impossible – would at some point have had a role in that breeding ground of Antipodean thespianism, the daily soap. Thus for weeks I had a diet of *Home and Away* and *Neighbours*. And thank goodness Glebe wasn't a woman or I would have had to add *Prisoner: Cell Block H* to the list . . .'

'And did he?' she asked.

Holmes nodded. 'It took me long enough to spot it. But there was one episode of *Neighbours* from 2003 with five minutes excised from the digital archive by some powerful entity. Not available anywhere – unless of course you could lay your hands on an original VHS recording, which features "Igor" in a small role as Nicholas Mason, a hapless sewer worker who suffers from necrotizing fasciitis . . .'

'My goodness!' exclaimed Adler. 'Even so, I did not approve of your inclusion on the case. I already had everything *entirely* under control. When the right moment came, I was always going to unleash Braithwaite. It's only a blessing that you didn't mess everything up for me.'

'Please!' I said. 'I implore you both. Take pity on one, seated at the same table, who is neither a master criminal nor a famous detective. And explain?'

The other two reluctantly tore their eyes from each other and considered me.

'The chair recognizes Ms Irene Adler,' said Holmes smoothly, with a magician's flourish.

'Let's get to the meat of the matter,' she said, as our steaks were laid in front of us. 'The rumours about EGO and where its medical expertise comes from: all true. There *were* illegal experimental surgeries done on the island of San Colombo. Many died. However, for those who didn't, the results were stunning. I speak with *personal knowledge.*'

'You mean . . . ?' said Holmes, horrified.

'Oh yes,' said Irene Adler. 'I was one of the lucky ones.'

34

Holmes and I gasped.

'You see, Moriarty knew the risks, but also the potential benefits. So he opened it up to an extremely select group of like-minded individuals . . .'

'. . . for that, read "scoundrels and criminals" . . .' muttered Holmes.

'. . . persons who inhabited a decidedly grey area of legality . . .' Adler went on.

'. . . as I suspected . . .'

'Oh, do stop interrupting, you ill-mannered schoolboy! You'll have your turn. Yes, okay – we were all confederates or business partners of the one known as Moriarty. I only worked for him occasionally – we had professional respect for each other. Although – note this – I *never* met him. He's still as mysterious to me as ever.'

'Fascinating!' I put in.

'He was utterly committed to this line of medical research. It was illegal to test, of course, but it *had* to be tested. He made us each an offer to be a guinea pig.'

'One can guess that the other invitees,' said Holmes, 'were the very individuals Braithwaite is now busily exposing.'

She nodded. 'So, for me – it worked. Astoundingly. My brain was rejuvenated, and my body followed suit. The treatment really is revolutionary. It's just a shame it can never get to market.'

'Why is that?' I asked.

Holmes and Adler both turned baleful stares upon me. A lump of steak fell off the end of my fork.

'Of course,' I said. 'Stupid me. Allowing Moriarty access to the insides of the brains of millions of people . . .'

'Perhaps to control them,' said Adler. 'Influence their political beliefs, surveil their every impulse, introduce subliminal advertising, maybe even erase memories . . .'

'Too horrible to imagine,' I agreed.

'Pray go on with the story,' said Holmes.

'I developed talents I'd never dreamed of,' said Adler. 'I became infinitely technologically proficient. I was like a sponge, and only needed two hours' sleep. I could hack into anything. One day I broke into Moriarty's own criminal mainframe just to see if I could. And that's when I glimpsed the crimes his other contacts got up to on a regular basis.

'Once I had found these things out, I could not unlearn them. And nor could I live with myself. The most unexpected thing had happened: I had developed a conscience.'

35

'I found out their names, and their addresses. It was difficult, long work, but rewarding. I ran scams on them, stole their money, gave it away to members of the public . . .'

'Particularly ingenious,' said Holmes, as our desserts arrived. 'You defaced their property, identified them to anyone who happened to connect the dots – and had Braithwaite as a back-up in case no one else managed to do it – and gave away their money, all at once . . .'

'And all the while remained anonymous. Magnificent!' I agreed.

'It was most gratifying,' Irene Adler conceded, rolling the wine around her glass. 'But then something happened. A few months ago, I noticed that the recently acquired mental acuity, the unstoppable energy, started to ebb. My brilliance was fading. But I had to make a final effort to stop Moriarty implementing his NEXT-GEN device – the effects of which would be catastrophic.

'I knew Moriarty ran EGO, and so this Igor Glebe fellow must be a fraud. I hoped that if I showed him what his employer was really up to, he'd be terrified – or more terrified than he was already – and want out. I was right. I gave him a virus to upload into the EGO mainframe. He did so . . .'

'I told you this was not one case but two, Watson,'

said Holmes, his eyes not leaving Adler, his voice hushed and reverent. 'The first case was a mere prison escape. Here we come to the second case: the greatest heist in history.'

'What! You don't mean it!' I said, turning to Adler.

'The disk I gave James Clement the actor was ransomware. I used it to retrieve all the medical research – much of which, of course, came from the illegal experiments. To get it back they would have to pay me a truly stupendous amount of Richstream. Just about all they've got left.'

'You recall Kostak and his security personnel running about like headless chickens,' said Holmes. 'Jenny Yuen told us that building normally had a dozen or so workers in it. That morning I counted sixty! They'd give anything to have that data back. Which allowed you to perform the largest robbery of all time.'

'That then turned into the smallest,' she said. 'Forty billion pounds' worth of cryptocurrency, which suddenly isn't enough to pay for this excellent glass of Barolo . . .'

'I wonder if they'll actually pay, after all,' said Holmes wonderingly.

'Oh, they did. This morning.'

Holmes sat up in his chair. 'They paid? Moriarty actually paid!'

'He had no choice,' said Adler, smiling into her wine glass. She took a luxuriant sniff and let it out slowly, looking out over the Thames.

'But that means – my god, of course! Moriarty will have to turn up to retrieve the disk when you hand it

back to him. There will be a chance to catch the scoun-
drel at last!'

'And I've given you a ringside seat,' said Adler. 'Because,
just in time as we finish these *splendid* desserts, here he
comes now . . .'

36

Holmes and I jumped to our feet, gripped the side of the boat, and stared upwards.

Above us loomed the Millennium Bridge. It was nearly on the stroke of midnight and a figure approached the middle, looking left and right. It was impossible to make out their age or appearance from the angle we were at.

They stopped at the centre, looking to first the north shore, then the south, trying vainly not to appear furtive.

A distant buzz sounded and a dark object came hovering into view, visible against the banks of lights on the buildings opposite.

I glanced at Irene Adler, who held in her lap a controller with a screen attached. She twisted the controls so that the figure on the bridge grew larger on the screen. I turned to the bridge and then back, momentarily unsure in which direction to look.

The drone lowered until it was within arm's reach, and the figure jumped up and caught it.

Then all hell broke loose. I realized I had been half-conscious for several moments of a deep subsonic throbbing, which now became the heavy thudding of the blades of four helicopters. Sirens howled from seemingly every direction. Blue and white lights reflected off water and glass, and teams of officers rappelled from their craft onto the bridge, guns raised, screaming instructions.

The figure did not hesitate.

In one bound they were over the edge. Two seconds of stunned silence, then there was a heavy splash in the glittering water, and they swam desperately – towards us.

Ernesto and the waiter pulled the figure from the water and hauled them spluttering onto the deck. In one hand was the disk they had retrieved. Holmes pulled back their hood while I stood ready, armed only with the restaurant's outsized pepper mill.

'If you won't bring a revolver, someone has to, Watson,' said Holmes, metal glinting in his hand. And then, viciously: 'Stand up, you!' The figure struggled to their feet.

'What does this mean?' I asked.

'A case of stolen or assumed identities,' said Holmes. The person before us was a boy of perhaps seventeen. 'Who the devil are you?' Holmes said.

The youth said something which I shall not repeat in print. In response to which, Holmes fired his revolver at the boy's feet.

'Holy shit!' said the boy. 'Watch what you're doing with that!'

'Señor!' said Ernesto. 'My boat!'

'Watson,' snarled Holmes, smoke still snaking from his revolver. 'Allow me to introduce Larian Moriarty – grandson of the master criminal!'

The boy spat on the floor. 'I'm better than he ever was,' he said.

'Apple doesn't fall far from the tree, does it, Watson?'

said Holmes, as a police motor launch pulled up alongside. 'Albeit occasionally it plops into the Thames. Better get some injections, you might have caught something nasty. Ah, here comes Lestrade . . .'

On first inspection the man appeared to be the
Republican candidate for the US Presidential Election

37

The referee was nine minutes late blowing the whistle to start the game between Tubmouth & Crettingdean and the Hengersham Dolphins. The delay was owing to an unaccustomed request for a press conference before the game with the home team's new manager, recently signed from Lazio.

Five reporters asked questions while the handsome and loquacious Italian gave forth. His translator, a short boulder-like woman with tightly bound ropes of grey hair, blinked a great deal as she condensed the information she had been given, before relaying it.

'Hengersham above us in league,' she said. 'But only two place above, and they have three points in last five games. Tubmouth improve week on week. We fresh as the fragrant basil on the margherita pizza at Geraldo's Ristorante – two-for-one Tuesdays – and improving with age like Geraldo's Chianti. Twenty per cent off for take-away, quote code "CRETINS". We confident. *Grazie, grazie*, is over, stop ask now . . .'

'I find myself rather peckish, Holmes,' I admitted, as the journalists were waved away and the gladiators took to the arena.

'I'm not surprised, Watson. Have you seen Geraldo's? It's been absolutely heaving since Geraldo's *nonna* took on her new role.'

'It's not the only place that's heaving,' I said, looking round.

'I know!' Holmes said jubilantly. 'Isn't it magnificent!'

What had formerly been a crowd of perhaps seventy had swelled to over three hundred. Temporary stands had been erected for the home supporters, and there was a feeling of crackling excitement. I sniffed, detecting something else in the air I found less delightful.

'What is that odour?' I asked. 'I recognize it . . .'

'Ah,' said Holmes. 'Do you not see the cans being drunk all around us? Free merchandise from the new sponsor . . . Fancy a tipple?' He held out a can of W.M.D.

'Holmes!' I protested. 'Aside from my own personal feelings, that is most certainly *not* a medicinal drink!' He chuckled, enjoying my discomfort, but squeezed my arm affectionately.

'I still have a few questions, Holmes,' I said a minute later, as two Hengersham players rose to meet a long pass, only to collide with Tubmouth defensive stalwart Dumughn with the sound of a paving slab landing in wet concrete.

'I thought Dumughn was off the team?' I asked, intrigued despite myself.

'So did I, but his tractor passed its MOT, to everyone's surprise, so he's able to make training again,' said Holmes with an insider's air.

'Tell me, Holmes – do you think Professor Moriarty perhaps still lives, despite everything?'

'I can't help feeling that Moriarty's academic credentials must have been rescinded by this point,' said Holmes testily, as Hengersham took a potshot from thirty yards that was tipped over the bar by Jim Clarke. 'Well done, Clarkie! Well done, son! Never seen a goalkeeper keep his glasses on through a match before – what a man. Anyhow, let's not worry about Moriarty, dead or alive. Let's enjoy the company of the living. Ah! Look who's over there!'

Holmes pointed out Jenny Yuen, who was cheering louder than anyone else, except for the woman next to her, who was in a wheelchair.

'Braithwaite's wife, Watson,' said Holmes. 'She's been able to get the best medical assistance since "Bitsy"' – here he winked – 'donated a million pounds to his coffers. And there's Braithwaite, playing left midfield for the Tubbers. He's not bad. Good eye for players in space. The Braithwaites enjoy it down here – the country air, you know.'

'This is marvellous,' I said. 'Will we not say hello to Ms Yuen? And I wonder where that actor fellow, James Clement, ended up . . .'

'I think we will leave her alone,' said Holmes. 'Seeing me would make her nervous. You see, I think she's happy. Yes – happy, I should say. It shines from her.'

'Why would you make her nervous?'

'Use your eyes, Watson. She is in love. I don't want to shatter her idyll. That's right, yes – now, out to Metcalf . . . Keep going, Metcalf . . .'

'Explain, Holmes! Please!'

'You see, the same time Glebe disappeared there was a mysterious new signing on the team. Tall, athletic, handsome – in a certain light you'd say he was Glebe's double. It's almost as though a man talented at disguising himself for years on end found a new role he far preferred.

Here he comes now! A cross comes in from Metcalf . . . The Ukrainian Dyskov rises to head it . . .'

A giant animal noise – that of three hundred human throats roaring – rippled into the sky as the Hengersham net billowed. Dark-haired Dyskov received the congratulations of his mobbing teammates, and for the tiniest moment, as he glanced towards the crowd, grinning from under his mop of black hair, he looked directly towards Jenny Yuen, and incidentally at us.

In a sea of cheering, jubilant, ecstatic people, suddenly all became clear.

'Who knows, Watson?' Holmes yelled into my ear over the noise of the crowd. 'We might win the Premier League yet!'

'Big talk, Holmes,' I replied. 'Enormous talk! Time will tell!'

'Touché, Watson! A point to you! Come on, you Tubby Cretins!'

Thanks

I really love these short Holmes and Watson books, but they are written to tight deadlines and I rely a lot on friends and loved ones for advice. It would be unspeakably rude for me not to thank those who've helped: Shyam Kumar and Max Edwards first, as editor and agent. Then Steve Savage, Evelyn Conn, Jim Clarke, Steve Dumughn, Paul Brann, Ben Metcalf, Patrick Ferguson, Dave McVey, Donnalyn Morris, John and Sally Why, Stuart Turner, Susan Dowdney, Alex Fedorec, Mark Richmond, Tom Vincent, Kate Hooper and Ben Vincent.

This little book is dedicated with huge fondness to Jon Appleton and Angela McMahon, and also to the memory of our beloved friend Thalia Proctor.